To my family

Copyright © 2021 by Nicolò Carozzi
All rights reserved. Published in the United States by Random House Studio,
an imprint of Random House Children's Books, a division of Penguin Random House LLC, New York.
Random House Studio and the colophon are registered trademarks of Penguin Random House LLC. • Visit us on
the Web! rhcbooks.com • Educators and librarians, for a variety of teaching tools, visit us at RHTeachersLibrarians.com

Library of Congress Cataloging-in-Publication Data is available upon request.
ISBN 978-0-593-18183-6 (trade) — ISBN 978-0-593-18184-3 (lib. bdg.) — ISBN 978-0-593-18185-0 (ebook)

The artist used graphite on paper with digital enhancing to create the illustrations for this book.
The text of this book is set in 28-point Garamond Premier Pro. • Design by Rachael Cole

MANUFACTURED IN CHINA
10 9 8 7 6 5 4 3 2
First Edition

BRAVE AS A MOUSE

NICOLÒ CAROZZI

RANDOM HOUSE STUDIO · NEW YORK

"Would you like to play?"
Mouse asked the fish.

"YES!"
the fish answered.

And so they did.

But then . . .

three others wanted to play, too.

But
Mouse
had
an idea.

It was a wild idea.

It was a bold idea.

It was a brave idea.

But was it a good idea?

It was not.

Fortunately, the cats found
something tastier.

All that eating made them sleepy,
but Mouse knew they would
not sleep forever.

Mouse had
another idea.

It was a wild idea.

It was a bold idea.

It was a brave idea.

"Are you ready?"
Mouse asked.

"YES!"

the fish answered.

Was it a good idea?

Yes, it was!